LOOSE TOOTH

by Steven Kroll

illustrated by Tricia Tusa

SCHOLASTIC INC.

New York Toronto London Auckland Sydney

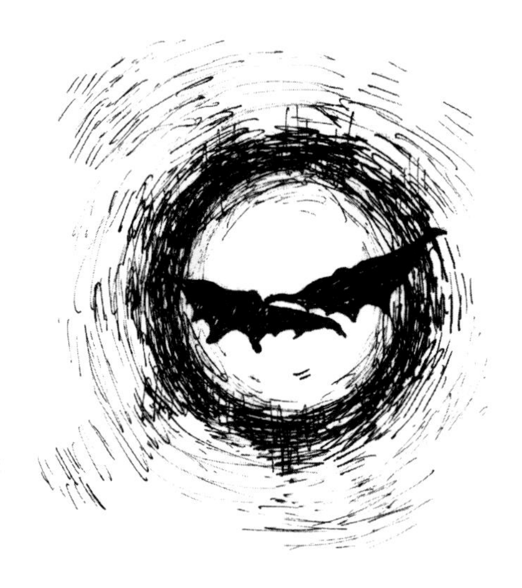

ISBN 0-590-45713-6

 Published by Scholastic Inc., 730 Broadway, New York, NY 10003, by arrangement with Holiday House, Inc.

12 11 10 9 8 7 6 3 4 5 6 7/9

Printed in the U.S.A. 08

First Scholastic printing, October 1992

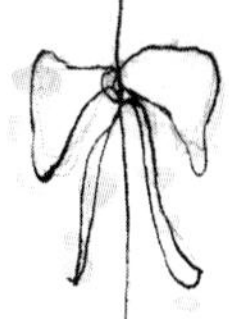

for Karen Ann, *who brings me joy.*

S.K.

for Fran, Theo, Sally, Nancy, *and* Eloise.

T.T.

Fangs and Flapper were twins. Everything they did, they did together.

When Fangs soared through the night sky, Flapper soared after him.

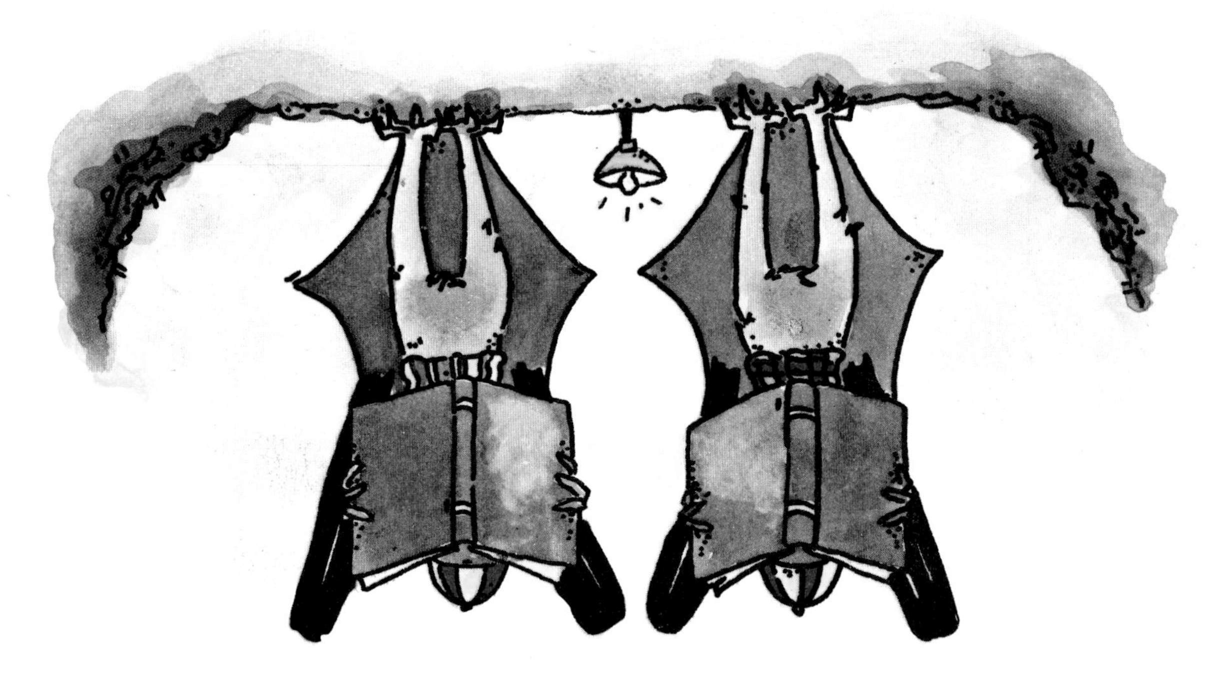

When Flapper read, Fangs read, too.

And when the other bats played flying football, Fangs and Flapper always joined them.

One day, in the middle of reading class, Fangs discovered he had a loose tooth. He felt the tooth with his tongue. It was very wiggly.

After class, Fangs showed Flapper. Then he showed his friends.

"Wow!" said Lizzy Lizard. "That tooth's going to fall out any minute!"

"You'll get lots of money from the tooth fairy when it does," said Henry Hawk.

Flapper felt around in his own mouth. He wanted to have a loose tooth like Fangs. But he didn't have one.

At recess, all the other animals crowded around Fangs and his loose tooth. Fangs was delighted. Every time someone came up to look, he did a loop-the-loop around the school yard.

The whole time, Flapper hung from the jungle gym. No one paid any attention to him at all.

That night at dinner, the tooth was looser.
"Be careful how you bite, dear," said Mom.
"You don't want to swallow it, Fangs," said Dad.
"I got a hundred on my spelling test," said Flapper.
But nobody paid attention. They were too busy looking at Fangs.

Fangs bit down on a piece of bread. Suddenly his tooth popped out of his mouth and landed in his soup.

Fangs was frantic. "Where is it?" he shouted. "I can't see it!"

"It's got to be in there somewhere," said Mom.

They all flapped around the bowl. Dad stuck in a claw and pulled out the tooth.

"Hooray!" shouted Fangs.
"Hooray!" shouted Dad.
"The tooth fairy comes tonight!" said Mom.

"I bet she's ugly," said Flapper.
But nobody even heard him.

After several family swoops around the neighborhood, it was time for bed.

"Remember the tooth fairy only comes when you're asleep," said Dad.

"I'm going to sleep right now," said Fangs.

He put the tooth on the ledge beside him.
He went to sleep, smiling.

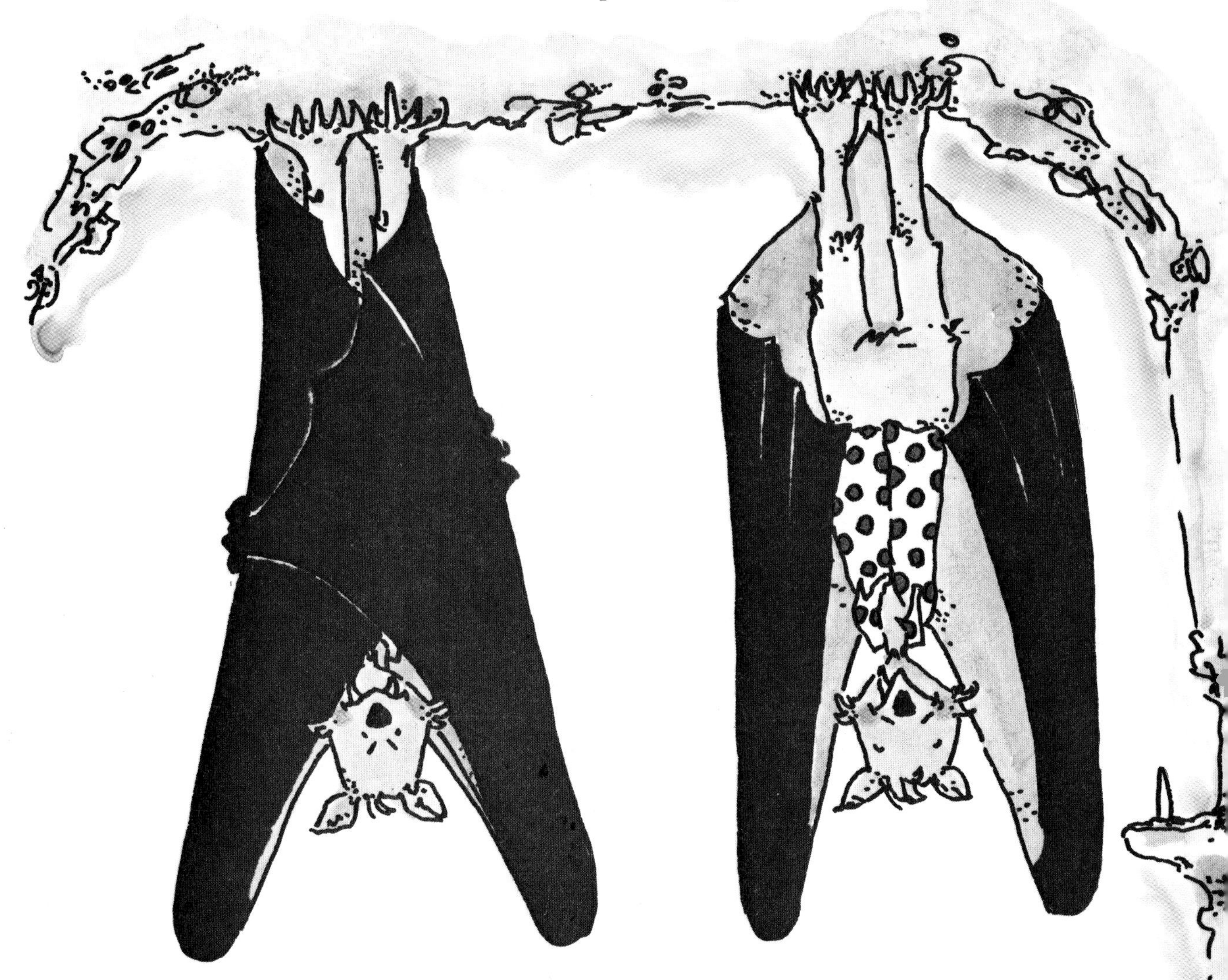

Nearby, Flapper hung frowning in the dark. Fangs has been getting all the attention, he thought, and I'm sick of it. I'm going to steal that stupid tooth!

Quietly he flew over to Fangs. Carefully he slipped the tooth off the ledge. Then he glided gently to the ground.

Now where could he hide the tooth? He didn't even have pockets. He flew to the kitchen.

Mom was already there! She was mixing the batter for some muffins.

Flapper was so surprised to see her, he dropped the tooth. Plop! It fell into the batter!

Flapper didn't know what to do. He hid on the ceiling.

RECIPES

Mom was so busy working, she hadn't noticed a thing. She finished mixing the batter and popped the muffins into the oven.

Oh, no! thought Flapper. The tooth's in a muffin!

Mom waited until the muffins were done. Then she flew back to her corner of the cave.

When Flapper was sure she wouldn't hear him, he glided back to his spot. But he couldn't sleep. Much later, he heard the flapping of wings near Fangs, followed by some grumbling. It must be the tooth fairy, he thought, as he finally dozed off.

In the morning, Flapper was stretching his wings when he heard Fangs screech, "The tooth fairy took my tooth and didn't leave me any money!"

Flapper shrugged.

At breakfast everyone was confused. "I'm sure the tooth fairy came," said Mom. "She probably couldn't find the tooth."

"But I left it for her," said Fangs.

"Maybe it fell on the ground," said Dad.

"It didn't," said Fangs. "I looked."

Flapper was much too worried to say anything. He'd tried two muffins. No tooth. Any minute, somebody would—

"Ouch!" said Mom. She pulled a piece of muffin out of her mouth. In it was the missing tooth.

"My tooth!" said Fangs.
"Goodness," said Mom.
"How did it get in the muffins?" asked Dad.

Flapper wiggled his wings nervously. Everyone looked at him. He knew he had to tell the truth.

When Flapper had told the whole story, Dad said, "Fangs, I'm giving you the quarter the tooth fairy would have left, but Flapper I'm giving you a quarter, too. We shouldn't have ignored you."

Flapper looked at Fangs. Fangs looked at Flapper. "You know what?" said Flapper.

"What?" said Fangs.

"My tooth feels loose."

"It does?" said Fangs. "How terrific! Let's go show our friends."

And the two of them flew off together.